Written by Melissa & Phil Sinatra
Illustrated by Melissa Sinatra

myscruffypuppy.com

ISBN 978-1-7337749-0-1

SCRUFFY PUPPy Gets a Bath

by Melissa and Phil Sinatra
illustrated by Melissa Sinatra

For Miller and Hurley

Kitty get up!
Something's going on.

Mom is filling up the bathtub and getting a bunch of towels.

This is so great! Everything is great!

I'm so excited.

 I'm going to write the best report ever.

I just have to find my crayons...

That Scruffy Puppy doesn't know what's going on, but I do.

No way I'm getting a bath. All that water soaking my handsome kitty fur.

No thank you.

I'm staying under here where it's warm and dry.

Oh boy! This is awesome. Kitty! Hurry up, you're going to miss all the fun.

There are bubbles everywhere, and the shampoo smells like strawberries.

That was so much fun. I love bubbles.

I can't wait for Kitty to play in the tub. He's going to have a blast.

He'll be swimming and playing with the bubbles in no time.

Kitties love water, right?

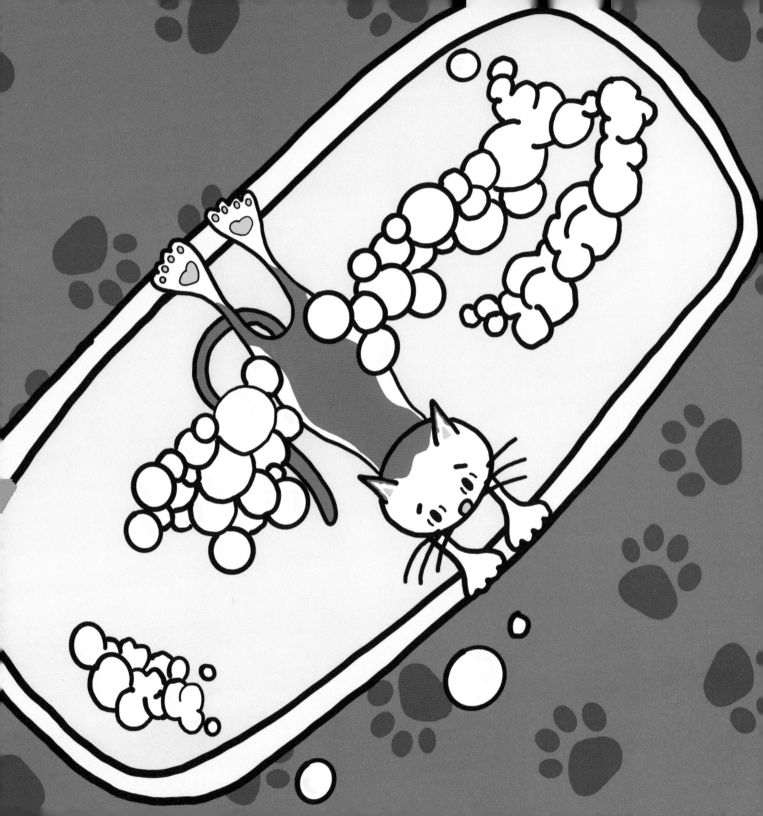

All that splashing around sure made me hungry.

Kitty must really be having a good time, he's late for dinner...

He's NEVER late for dinner, or any meal for that matter.

Did someone say dinner?

That Scruffy Puppy is eating delicious entrée and I'm in here, soaked to the bone? My delicate fur saturated. My handsome face covered in bubbles.

What have I done to deserve this?

What a great day! Dinner sure was yummy!

All that splashing and playing made me so sleepy. I think it's time for a puppy nap.

I wonder where Kitty is. He missed dinner and now he's missing nap time.

He must be having so much fun playing in the bathtub he doesn't want to get out.

He's such a funny guy.

This is ridiculous.

Printed in Great Britain
by Amazon

14032939R10020